VALENTINE'S DAY
COLORING BOOK
FOR BOYS

THIS COLORING BOOK BELONGS TO:

I DIG YOU

Small
Planet
Publishing

We are so thrilled you've chosen to purchase our product.
How are you liking it so far?
We are working hard to build a higher quality product
for our customers by listening to buyers' comments and concerns.

Thank you for your order
Please remember to leave us feedback!

Made in the USA
Coppell, TX
31 January 2025

45229363R00031